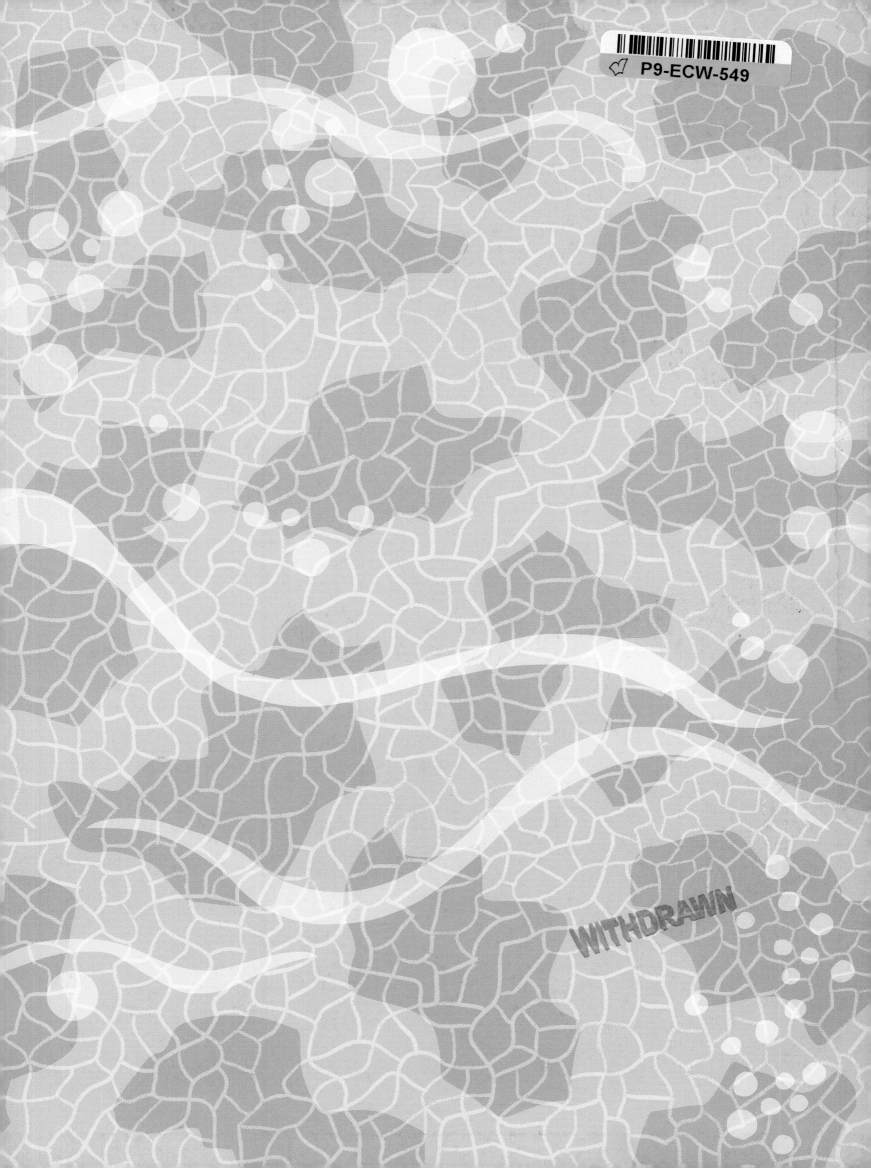

For Tiloune, fearless princess!
C. A.

To Fabienne,
for his painting skills on my blank canvass.
F. S.

© for the French edition: L' Élan vert, Saint-Pierre-des-Corps, 2018
Title of the original edition: Un dragon sur le toit
© for the English edition: Prestel Verlag, Munich • London • New York, 2019
A member of Verlagsgruppe Random House GmbH
Neumarkter Strasse 28 • 81673 Munich

For the photos: Antoni Gaudí, Casa Batlló, 1904–1906, in Barcelona, Spain.
Back cover and page 28: front of the building; page 29 top right:
detail of the roof.
© Casa Batlló S.L.U.
Page 29 top left: main stairs; page 29 below: living room of the grand
apartment.
© Bednorz Images / Bridgeman Images

Prestel Publishing Ltd.
14-17 Wells Street
London W1T 3PD

Prestel Publishing
900 Broadway, Suite 603
New York, NY 10003

Library of Congress Control Number: 2018965314
A CIP catalogue record for this book is available from the British Library.

Translated from the French by Paul Kelly
Copyediting: Brad Finger
Project management: Melanie Schöni
Production management and typesetting: Susanne Hermann
Printing and binding: TBB, a.s.

MIX
From responsible
sources
FSC® C022120

Verlagsgruppe Random House FSC® N001967

Printed in Slovakia
ISBN 978-3-7913-7391-1
www.prestel.com

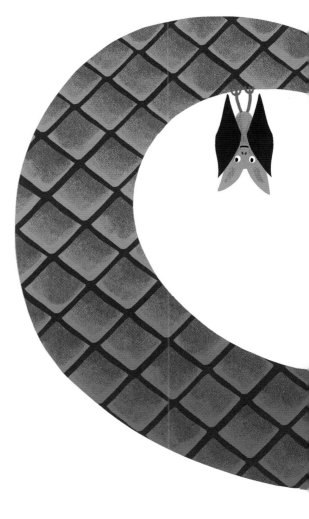

A DRAGON ON THE ROOF

A Children's Book
Inspired by Antoni Gaudí

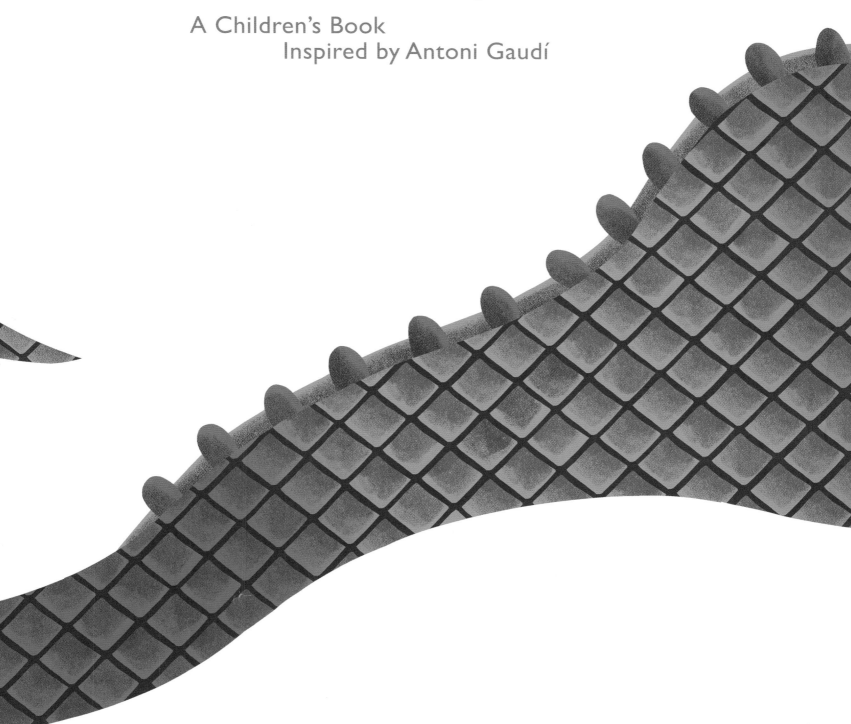

PRESTEL

Munich · London · New York

Paloma is bored sitting in front of the fireplace. Doña Rosa, her elderly nanny, is falling asleep. "Stop fidgeting," she had told her, "you have to be a good girl, a buena chica!" But now the old woman has begun to snore, her chin resting on her bodice. Suddenly, a glint appears in Paloma's eyes.

Outside, the sky grows dark and the sun disappears. The wind is on the rise, and the leaves are swirling around in clusters! What is that roaring in the distance? Is it a storm, a tempest, a tornado? All of a sudden, Paloma is startled by an odd creature that, with every last bit of strength in its tiny paws, is banging against the window pane. "Who are you?," marvels the child as she opens the window. **"It's the bat, of course!"**

Rushing inside, it flies about, bangs into something and appears quite distressed. "It's chasing me! What a disaster, what a catastrophe!," moans the bat. Paloma takes the animal in her hands and presses it against her heart. "Shush, shush… calm down. **What's happening?** Who are you afraid of?" No sooner has she uttered these words than the walls begin to tremble.

She does not notice the jagged shapes pressing into the walls, the door handles that twist like snake's tongues and the stairway that curves like an animal's spine. Paloma just runs! She wants to find out who has come into her house, and what that intruder could want!

"It's over there, in the corridor. Let's catch it!" Paloma flies at full speed from one room to the next. "He'll bite us!," screams the bat in panic. "I hear a noise in the living room!," says the young girl. "Let's go before he wakes Doña Rosa!" In the fireplace, the fire has gone out. The nanny is still snoring, but there are three blood-red scales at her feet and a **gigantic** mark made by long claws!

Paloma is off and running again — she loves dragons! "Come back, he'll de… de… devour you!" stutters the bat, completely terrified. The little girl is not afraid. She hunts around the kitchen and bounces from room to room, finding nothing. Paloma then climbs up to the attic, pushes open the door and tip-toes in. She hears a heart pounding —

thud, thud, thud!

Paloma reaches out with her hand and feels the cold skin of the creature beneath her. "Oh, my beauty, my lovely. Let me stroke you," she whispers. She gently scratches between its scales. Doesn't she know that dragons are sensitive to tickling?

Then, out of nowhere, the dragon explodes with laughter… unleashing the sea and all its waves, tuna, crabs, cuttlefish and seaweed! The house becomes **a giant aquarium**, with water running up to the porch. Driven on by the waves, the bat splashes about. "Help me!," it gurgles. A giant sea turtle and a wall of sardines eventually save the bat and guide it back up to the roof.

"Well, you could have spat them out somewhere else!," scolds Paloma.
"Are you happy about flooding the house?"
"I'm sorry!," says the dragon, brushing his eye, "what I need is sleep, sleep and more sleep... I don't suppose you would have somewhere for me to sleep?" He stretches out his body and **opens his mouth wide.**

Little Paloma drags the huge animal into a corner. The bat, having calmed down a bit, hums out a tune to remind him of faraway caves. The dragon closes its eyes and falls asleep. Reassured, the sun starts to shine. And without a sound, Paloma returns to sit in front of the fireplace.

As soon as Paloma is settled, her nanny wakes up. "Are you well, muchacha?," she asks. "Perfectly well," replies the child. "I dozed off," sighs Doña Rosa, placing her glasses on her nose. "Everything is so calm today!" The old nanny begins to light up the fire, when her eyes suddenly open wide. **"But, what's this?,"** she exclaims.

Between her thumb and forefinger she holds a tiny seahorse, which is quivering angrily. "Oh, a seahorse that has lost its way," says Paloma. She takes it and puts it discreetly into a vase that is overflowing with seawater. Doña Rosa looks at the ceiling and runs her hand over the walls. "That's strange. **I get the feeling that everything is scratched and scraped here. I don't recognize anything anymore."** "Maybe you need new glasses," declares the little girl.

The old lady shrugs. "There is something not quite right about this house," she says as she stokes up the fire. A mischievous flicker appears in Paloma's eyes. Under the bench, the bat gently laughs. "Poor Doña Rosa! What is she going to say when she finds out there is **a dragon on the roof?!**"

ANTONI GAUDÍ

Building constructed
from 1904 – 1906
in Barcelona, Spain

CASA BATLLÓ

Façade of the building

Detail of the roof

Details of the main stairwell

Living room of the grand apartment

ANTONI GAUDÍ

A MODERN CATALAN ARCHITECT

Antoni Gaudí is to Barcelona what the Eiffel Tower is to Paris: inseparable. As the Catalan capital grew rich and expanded towards the end of the 19th century, wealthy families began commissioning architects to build new homes. Gaudí used his commissions to create revolutionary buildings. In earlier centuries, architects had worked to achieve perfect proportions and symmetry. Their efforts can be seen in everything from the temples of ancient Greece to the Palace of Versailles. Breaking from this established tradition, Gaudí used ideas from the Art Nouveau movement, designing architecture with asymmetrical curves and swirling forms that one finds in nature. He also combined industrial materials, such as steel, glass, ceramics, etc., with such traditional materials as stone and wood. Gaudí used all of these components, along with a few clever tricks, to create his own Catalan take on modern architecture. His buildings would be functional and, at the same time, offer beauty and fantasy to their inhabitants.

CASA BATLLÓ

This narrow house is located at number 43 du Passeig de Gràcia. It probably looked like other "normal" homes in 1877, when it was first completed. By 1903, however, the building had been purchased by a wealthy textile manufacturer, Josep Batlló Casanovas, and he wanted to have it completely refurbished. Gaudí went to work on this project between 1904 and 1906. On the ground floor level, striking elephant-shaped columns give the illusion of grandness. Above, the upper floors are adorned with curving balconies, small flat disks that resemble fish scales, and glistening mosaic pieces. Draped over all of this is a fanciful roof with bluish and pink tiles and chimneys with colorful ceramic fragments. Sweeping through the inside of the house are undulating walls and ceilings that have neither corners nor edges, neither straight lines nor flat surfaces. They seem to be sculpted out of stone!

THE STORY BEHIND THE HOUSE

Gaudí was inspired my marine life, which would explain the prevalence of blue hues in his work. The idea of a dragon may have come from a folk tale, well known in Catalonia, where St. George slays a dragon. On closer inspection, one can see that the elongated shapes of the façade and the stairways are meant to resemble animal bones. That's why the Casa Batlló is known in Barcelona as the "Casa de los Huesos," or the House of Bones! Finally, up on the roof, the scaly back of a dragon can be seen. A cross atop the tower represents the point of the spear that St. George used to pierce the dragon's body. This is something new in architecture: a house that tells a story!

WHERE CAN WE FIND GAUDI'S BUILDINGS?

In Barcelona, of course! The Casa Milá, Güell Palace, Park Güell and Casa Batlló: all of these masterpieces have been granted world heritage status by the United Nations Educational, Scientific and Cultural Organization, or UNESCO. Another world heritage building is the Sagrada Familia (Holy Family), the basilica to which Gaudi dedicated a large part of his life. When he died in 1926, only the church's crypt, apse and façade of the nativity had been completed… and the building is still under construction in 2019!